La galletita

The Little Cookie

El hombre de galleta de jengibre/The Gingerbread Man
Contado por/Retold by Margaret Hillert
Ilustrado por/Illustrated by Steven James Petruccio

NORWOOD HOUSE PRESS

Querido padre o tutor: Es posible que los libros de esta serie para lectores principiantes les resulten familiares, ya que las versiones originales de los mismos podrían haber formado parte de sus primeras lecturas. Estos textos, cuidadosamente escritos, incluyen palabras de uso frecuente que le proveen al niño la oportunidad de familiarizarse con las más comúnmente usadas en el lenguaje escrito. Estas nuevas versiones han sido actualizadas y las encantadoras ilustraciones son sumamente atractivas para una nueva generación de pequeños lectores.

Primero, léale el cuento al niño, después permita que él lea las palabras con las que esté familiarizado, y pronto podrá leer solito todo el cuento. En cada paso, elogie el esfuerzo del niño para que desarrolle confianza como lector independiente. Hable sobre las ilustraciones y anime al niño a relacionar el cuento con su propia vida.

Al final del cuento, encontrará actividades relacionadas con la lectura que ayudarán a su niño a practicar y fortalecer sus habilidades como lector. Estas actividades, junto con las preguntas de comprensión, se adhieren a los estándares actuales, de manera que la lectura en casa apoyará directamente los objetivos de instrucción en el salón de clase.

Sobre todo, la parte más importante de toda la experiencia de la lectura es ¡divertirse y disfrutarla!

Dear Caregiver: The books in this Beginning-to-Read collection may look somewhat familiar in that the original versions could have been a part of your own early reading experiences. These carefully written texts feature common sight words to provide your child multiple exposures to the words appearing most frequently in written text. These new versions have been updated and the engaging illustrations are highly appealing to a contemporary audience of young readers.

Begin by reading the story to your child, followed by letting him or her read familiar words and soon your child will be able to read the story independently. At each step of the way, be sure to praise your reader's efforts to build his or her confidence as an independent reader. Discuss the pictures and encourage your child to make connections between the story and his or her own life.

At the end of the story, you will find reading activities that will help your child practice and strengthen beginning reading skills. These activities, along with the comprehension questions are aligned to current standards, so reading efforts at home will directly support the instructional goals in the classroom.

Above all, the most important part of the reading experience is to have fun and enjoy it!

Shannon Cannon

Shannon Cannon, Ph.D., Consultora de lectoescritura / Literacy Consultant

Norwood House Press • www.norwoodhousepress.com
Beginning-to-Read ™ is a registered trademark of Norwood House Press.
Illustration and cover design copyright ©2018 by Norwood House Press. All Rights Reserved.

Authorized Bilingual adaptation from the U.S. English language edition, entitled The Little Cookie by Margaret Hillert. Copyright © 2017 Margaret Hillert. Bilingual adaptation Copyright © 2018 Margaret Hillert. Translated and adapted with permission. All rights reserved. Pearson and La galletita are trademarks, in the US and/or other countries, of Pearson Education, Inc. or its affiliates. This publication is protected by copyright, and prior permission to re-use in any way in any format is required by both Norwood House Press and Pearson Education. This book is authorized in the United States for use in schools and public libraries.j32

Designer: Ron Jaffe   •   Editorial Production: Lisa Walsh

LIBRARY OF CONGRESS CATALOGING-IN-PUBLICATION DATA
Names: Hillert, Margaret, author. | Petruccio, Steven, illustrator. | Del
   Risco, Eida, translator. | Hillert, Margaret. Little cookie. | Hillert,
   Margaret. Little cookie. Spanish.
Title: La galletita = The little cookie / por Margaret Hillert ; ilustrado
   por Steven James Petruccio ; traducido por Eida Del Risco.
Other titles: Gingerbread boy. English.
Description: Chicago Illinois : Norwood House Press, [2017] | Series: A
   beginning-to-read book | Summary: "An easy to read fairy tale about The
   Gingerbread Man who avoids being eaten. Spanish/English edition includes
   reading activities"-- Provided by publisher.
Identifiers: LCCN 2016057970 (print) | LCCN 2017018260 (ebook) | ISBN
   9781684040599 (eBook) | ISBN 9781599538457 (library edition : alk. paper)
Subjects: | CYAC: Folklore. | Spanish language materials–Bilingual.
Classification: LCC PZ74.1 (ebook) | LCC PZ74.1 .H543 2017 (print) | DDC
   398.2 [E] --dc23
LC record available at https://lccn.loc.gov/2016057970

Hardcover ISBN: 978-1-59953-845-7   Paperback ISBN: 978-1-68404-044-5

302N—072017
Manufactured in the United States of America in North Mankato, Minnesota.

Mira como trabajo.
Puedo hacer algo.
Puedo hacer una galletita,
una galletita graciosa.

See me work.
I can make something.
I can make a cookie,
a funny little cookie.

Mira, mira.
Mira la galletita graciosa.
Es pequeña.

Look, look.
See the funny cookie.
It is little.

Ay, mira.
Mira como se va.
Puede correr y saltar.
Se puede escapar.

Oh, look.
See it go.
It can run and jump.
It can run away.

No, no, galletita.
Vuelve. Vuelve.
Te quiero.

No, no, little cookie.
Come here. Come here.
I want you.

No, no.
Mira como me voy.
Puedo correr y jugar.
Me puedo escapar.
No me puedes atrapar.

No, no.
See me go.
I can run and play.
I can run away.
You can not get me.

Es divertido correr.
Es divertido jugar.
Puedo correr y correr.
Me puedo escapar.

It is fun to run.
It is fun to play.
I can run, run, run.
I can run away.

Puedo subir.

I can go up.

Puedo bajar.
Lejos, lejos, lejos.

I can go down.
Away, away, away.

Galletita, galletita.
Ven aquí.
Ven aquí conmigo.
Te quiero.

Cookie, cookie.
Come here.
Come here to me.
I want you.

No, no.
Mira como me voy.
Puedo correr y jugar.
Me puedo escapar.
No me puedes atrapar.

No, no.
See me go.
I can run and play.
I can run away.
You can not get me.

Mira arriba, galletita.
Mira aquí arriba.
Ven a mí.
Te quiero.

Look up, cookie.
Look up here.
Come to me.
I want you.

No, no.
Mira como me voy.
Puedo correr y jugar.
Me puedo escapar.
No me puedes atrapar.

No, no.
See me go.
I can run and play.
I can run away.
You can not get me.

Mira aquí abajo, galletita.
Mira aquí abajo.
Entra en mi casa.
Te quiero.

Look down, cookie.
Look down here.
Come into my house.
I want you.

No, no.
Mira como me voy.
Puedo correr y jugar.
Me puedo escapar.
No me puedes atrapar.

No, no.
See me go.
I can run and play.
I can run away.
You can not get me.

Galletita, galletita.
Mira qué grande soy.
Te quiero.
Ven conmigo.

Cookie, cookie.
See big me.
I want you.
Come here to me.

No, no.
Mira como me voy.
Puedo correr y jugar.
Me puedo escapar.
No me puedes atrapar.

No, no.
See me go.
I can run and play.
I can run away.
You can not get me.

Ven aquí, galletita.
Te quiero.
Corre, corre, corre.
Corre hasta donde estoy.

Come here, little cookie.
I want you.
Run, run, run.
Run here to me.

No, no.
Mira como me voy.
Puedo correr y jugar.
Me puedo escapar.
No me puedes atrapar.

No, no.
See me go.
I can run and play.
I can run away.
You can not get me.

Ay, ay.
No puedo ir ahí.
No puedo entrar ahí.

Oh, my.
I can not go here.
I can not go in here.

Ven conmigo, galletita.
Yo puedo ayudarte.
Yo puedo entrar.

Come to me, little cookie.
I can help you.
I can go in.

Uno, dos y tres.
¡Ahí vamos!

One, two, three.
Here we go!

¡Ay, no! ¡Ay, no!
Mírame ahora.
¿Qué pasa?
Esto no es bueno.
¡No, esto no es bueno!

Oh, no! Oh, no!
Look at me now.
What is this?
This is not good.
No, this is not good!

Foundational Skills

In addition to reading the numerous high-frequency words in the text, this book also supports the development of foundational skills.

Phonological Awareness: The /k/ sound made with c

Oral Blending: Explain to your child that sometimes the letter **c** makes the same sound as **k**. Say the beginning and ending sounds of the following words and ask your child to listen to the sounds and say the whole word:

/k/ + at = cat	/k/ + ab = cab	/k/ + ane = cane
/k/ + ow = cow	/k/ + oat = coat	/k/ + an = can
/k/ + old = cold	/k/ + amp = camp	/k/ + ub = cub

Phonics: The letter Cc

1. Demonstrate how to form the letters **C** and **c** for your child.
2. Have your child practice writing **C** and **c** at least three times each.
3. Ask your child to point to the words in the book that start with the letter **c.**
4. Write down the following words and ask your child to circle the letter **c** in each word:

can	carry	cookie	pack	cat	come
case	rack	car	tractor	sack	cracker

Fluency: Refrain

1. Reread the story to your child at least two more times while your child tracks the print by running a finger under the words as they are read. Ask your child to read the words he or she knows with you.
2. The sentences on page 9 are called a refrain because they are repeated throughout the story. Read the refrain to your child, stopping after each sentence to allow your child to echo you.
3. Help your child practice reading the entire refrain.
4. Reread the story, stopping at pages that have the refrain to let your child read it. Encourage your child to read with expression.

Language

The concepts, illustrations, and text help children develop language both explicitly and implicitly.

Vocabulary: Verbs

1. Explain to your child that words that describe actions are called verbs.
2. Ask your child to name as many action words (verbs) as possible. Write the words on separate pieces of paper
3. Read each word to your child and ask your child to repeat it.
4. Mix the words up. Point to a word and ask your child to read it. Provide clues if your child needs them.
5. Read the following sentences to your child. Ask your child to provide an appropriate verb to complete the sentence.

   - The woman in the story _____ a cookie.
   - The cookie could _____ and _____.
   - At school, we _____ lots of books.
   - I like to _____ outside with my friends.

Reading Literature and Informational Text

To support comprehension, ask your child the following questions. The answers either come directly from the text or require inferences and discussion.

Key Ideas and Detail

- Ask your child to retell the sequence of events in the story.
- What animals wanted to get the Little Cookie?

Craft and Structure

- Is this a book that tells a story or one that gives information? How do you know?
- Could this story really happen? Why or why not?

Integration of Knowledge and Ideas

- Why did Little Cookie need help to get across the water?
- What is the lesson in the story?

Photograph by Glenna Washburn

ACERCA DE LA AUTORA

Margaret Hillert ha ayudado a millones de niños de todo el mundo a aprender a leer independientemente. Fue maestra de primer grado por 34 años y durante esa época empezó a escribir libros con los que sus estudiantes pudieran ganar confianza en la lectura y pudieran, al mismo tiempo, disfrutarla. Ha escrito más de 100 libros para niños que comienzan a leer. De niña, disfrutaba escribiendo poesía y, de adulta, continuó su escritura poética tanto para niños como para adultos.

ABOUT THE AUTHOR

Margaret Hillert has helped millions of children all over the world learn to read independently. She was a first grade teacher for 34 years and during that time started writing books that her students could both gain confidence in reading and enjoy. She wrote well over 100 books for children just learning to read. As a child, she enjoyed writing poetry and continued her poetic writings as an adult for both children and adults.

ACERCA DEL ILUSTRADOR

Steven James Petruccio ha ilustrado más de setenta álbumes para niños. Ha recibido el premio *Parent's Choice* y el premio *Rip VanWinkle* por su contribución a la literatura infantil. Steven y su familia viven en el hermoso valle del Hudson, donde encuentra inspiración para su obra.

ABOUT THE ILLUSTRATOR

Steven James Petruccio is the illustrator of more than seventy picture books. He has received *Parent's Choice Awards* and *The Rip VanWinkle Award* for his contribution to children's literature. Steven and his family live in the beautiful Hudson Valley which inspires his work.